Utterly Flutterly Fairies

Daisy
the
Dream Fairy

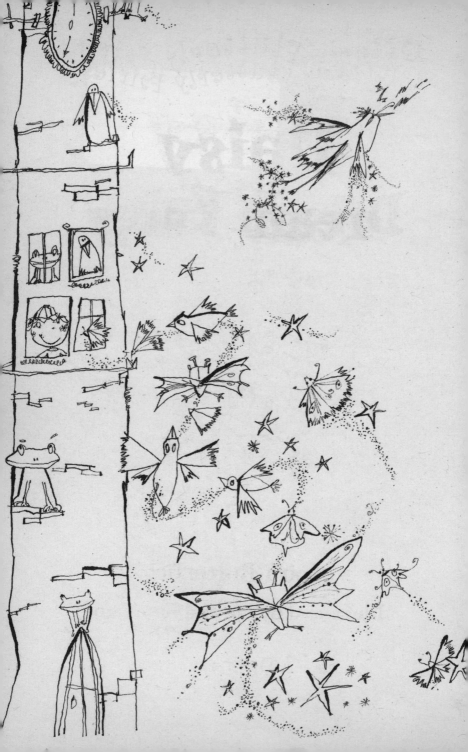

Utterly Flutterly Fairies

Daisy
the
Dream Fairy

Moira Butterfield

Illustrated by Liz and Kate Pope

Freya's home

Daisy's home

Human School

Fairy Scho

Clara's home

Windmill Wood

Human town

rubbish du

Seashell Beach

Meet the Utterly Flutterly Fairies!

Daisy the Dream Fairy

Special spells in her backpack

Clever weather magic dust
The power to calm storms

Magic beauty jewel
The power to create starlight

A good feeling spell ring
The power to make everything taste dreamy

Daisy's special skill
*She is able to fly very fast
and she is good at sport*

Freya the Fashion Fairy

Special spells in her backpack

Clever weather magic dust
The power to make a rainbow

Magic beauty jewel
The power to create beautiful clothes

A good feeling spell ring
The power to give someone a happy thought

Freya's special skill
*She is able to camouflage herself,
so people don't see her*

Clara the Clever Fairy

Special spells in her backpack

Clever weather magic dust
*The power to create a gentle breeze
(No wonder her Dad is always
inventing new kinds of windmill
to help run their home)*

Magic beauty jewel
The power to change colours

A good feeling spell ring
The power to give someone a bright idea

Clara's special skill
*She can make objects move a little (she's still
learning how to make them move a lot). She
can also magically see where things are broken*

Sophie the Birthday Fairy

Special spells in her backpack

Clever weather magic dust
The power to conjure up some sunshine

Magic beauty jewel
The power to make someone hear beautiful music

A good feeling spell ring
The power to put a smile on someone's face

Sophie's special skill
*She is especially good at looking after
animals, and can talk their languages*

And watch out for...

Drizzle the Wicked Witch

She would just love to get her hands on the fairies' spells, with the help of her mean and horrible sidekicks, the Craggy Crows!

More Utterly Flutterly Fun!

Look out for the pages of Utterly Flutterly Fairy Fun at the end of this book.

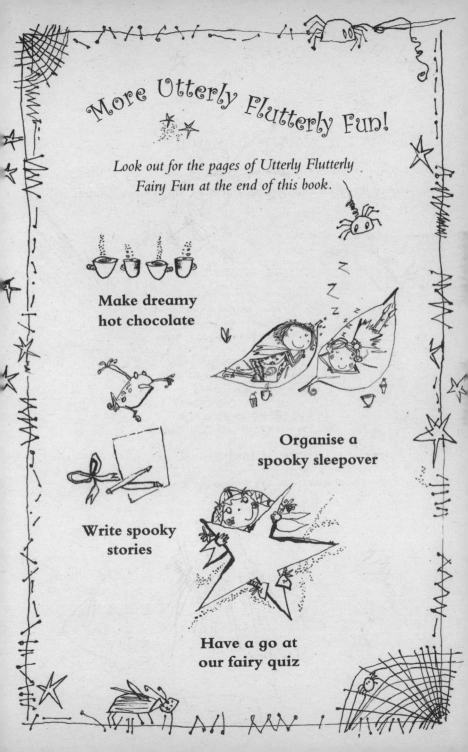

**Make dreamy
hot chocolate**

**Organise a
spooky sleepover**

**Write spooky
stories**

**Have a go at
our fairy quiz**

Written by Moira Butterfield
Designed by Tracey Cunnell
Edited by Pat Hegarty
Illustrated by Liz and Kate Pope

Created by WizzBook Ltd
Copyright © 2009 WizzBook Ltd
All rights reserved.

First published in the UK
by Potter Books, RH17 5PA, UK

www.potterbooks.co.uk

Printed in the UK by CPI Bookmarque, Croydon, CR0 4TD

Chapter 1
Night School

The next time you go to your school, look carefully around the playground. Is there a quiet spot in a corner? Could something small, secret and magical be hiding there? I heard that in a hole in a tree, on the edge of somebody's school playground, there was a very special secret indeed – the *Utterly Flutterly Fairy School*! I don't know which playground it's in. It could be yours. If you spot it, keep it a secret, won't you?

Little fairies arrive at the fairy school every morning, just after the human children have gone indoors. Occasionally, Daisy the Dream Fairy gets to school a bit late, but the head teacher, Mrs Daffodil, doesn't mind. She understands that Dream Fairies are nighttime fairies really, so waking up early in the morning can be hard for them.

Daisy lives with her Dream Fairy family in an old clock tower by Moonbeam Lake. Her four little pet bats – Itsy, Bitsy, Batso and Bottletop – take it in turns to give her a lift to school. All she has to do is hold on tightly and try not to yawn too much!

Come on, Bottletop!

One morning, Bitsy gave Daisy a gentle nudge to wake her up in time for class that day. Daisy yawned and then snuggled back down under her bedcovers.

"It's alright, Bitsy," she explained. "I forgot to tell you, I don't have to go to school today. Our class is having a moonlit flying lesson tonight, instead. And guess where it's going to be? Here at Moonbeam Lake! That means we can go back to sleep, Bitsy."

And that's just what she did.

That evening, the whole of Daisy's class arrived at Moonbeam Lake, including Daisy's three best friends – Freya, Clara and Sophie. Lots of animals lived around the lake, and some of them had come out to see the fairies. Silvery moths and tiny, glowing fireflies buzzed around.

Every now and again, a wild bat would flit through the trees.

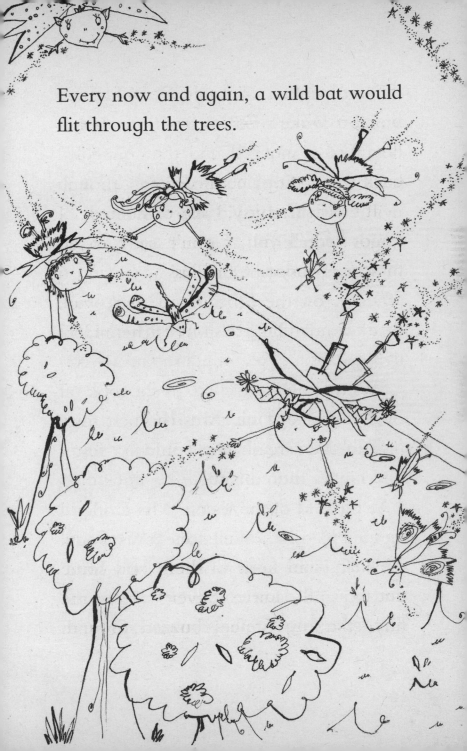

Freya sighed, happily. "Ohhh, no wonder Dream Fairies live here. It's so beautiful at night."

Clara and Sophie both agreed, though neither of them could stop yawning.

"It's wonderful…yawn…sorry, it's a bit late for us to be up."

Daisy, on the other hand, was wide awake and itching to show off her night-flying skills.

"Watch me!" she cried, as she took off over the lake. Daisy was the best fairy flier in the school. She could go faster and higher than anyone.

At the end of the lesson, Mrs Daffodil seemed pleased. "Well done, everybody! This class has been working very hard, and you all deserve a treat." Then she handed a sheet of paper to each fairy, to show their parents.

Daisy read it out loud, as her friends gathered around.

"School trip to Silvershell Bay.

The human school is going on a camping trip to the seaside. We would like to go along, with this class of fairies. We will learn lots of new things and we can keep an eye on the humans, to make sure they stay happy."

Everybody was delighted.

"Seaside, here we come!" Daisy cried. She was so excited that she flew up into the air and did a loop-the-loop!

Chapter 2

Silvershell Bay

On the morning of the trip, the fairies arrived at school as usual.

Mrs Daffodil told them what was going to happen. "We'll wait for the humans to leave on their trip and then we'll follow."

They watched out of the fairy school windows as, down below them in the playground, the human children waved goodbye to their parents and climbed on to a coach. Some of the youngest children in the school were going.

"It's our job to make sure the human children stay safe and well," Mrs Daffodil explained. "We need to keep a special eye on the little ones. They may never have been away from home before, and they might feel homesick. So, make sure you all bring your backpacks with your special spells inside. You may be needing them at Silvershell Bay."

As soon as the big school coach had pulled away, the fairies clambered on to their very own fairy bus – an empty bird's nest, pulled along by rainbow-coloured beetles. Mrs Daffodil pointed into the distance as the beetles flapped their wings and the bus rose into the air.

"Take us to Silvershell Bay!"

"To the sea!" the fairies all cried.

When they arrived, they saw that the human school coach was parked at a campsite by the beach. The children were all helping to put up tents.

Mrs Daffodil led the fairies into a patch of tall wild flowers on the edge of the site. "We'll camp here, where nobody can see us. First, we must collect some leaves," she ordered.

The fairies hurried off to hunt under nearby trees. Soon they returned, carrying leaves of all different shapes and sizes. Mrs Daffodil raised a hand and chanted a spell:

"Make some tents upon the ground,
To keep the fairies safe and sound."

The leaves stirred, fluttered and magically began to dance. Then they lined up in groups and slowly bowed to each other, arching over to make perfect fairy tents.

Daisy, Freya, Clara and Sophie lined the floor of their tent with soft moss and found some petals to make sheets and pillows. As soon as they had finished getting everything ready, they rushed down to Silvershell Beach.

Freya began hunting around on the soft sand. "I'm going to collect enough shells to make a necklace. That's what we Fashion Fairies do at the seaside!"

Clara laughed. "I'm going to work out how to make a great sandcastle. That's what we Clever Fairies do when we're at the seaside!"

Sophie had her own plan. "I'm going to paddle. When we Birthday Fairies are at the seaside, we have as much fun as we can! What do Dream Fairies do, Daisy?"

Daisy grinned. "You can see later on, if you can stay awake."

The sun shone, the sea swished gently, and it seemed like a perfect day.

But, had the fairies looked up, they might have caught a glimpse of a spoilsport.

A Craggy Crow had seen the humans setting up their campsite, and he was soon on his way home to Stinky Swamp to tell Drizzle the Wicked Witch.

What a wonderful witchy idea it would be to ruin someone's holiday!

Chapter 3
Scary Shadows

Drizzle was in Stinky Swamp, pouring nasty things into her cauldron of potion. This time, she was adding rotten cabbage juice mixed with curdled milk. She was always testing new ingredients, all of them yucky, to try to make the potion stronger. She couldn't understand why it was always so weak and useless for making mean magic.

The real reason was that Mrs Daffodil had put a spell on the witch's cauldron.

Her secret enchantment only stopped working when there was chaos and unhappiness in the human world. Then, the potion seemed to suck power from the air and grow strong. It would begin to bubble up and Drizzle could use it to make her magic.

Luckily, the potion's power never lasted long, but the witch was always trying to think of ideas to make it stronger. That meant she was always trying to work out ways to make people unhappy.

Drizzle shrieked when the Craggy Crow told her what he'd seen at Silvershell Bay.

"How stupid those humans are! I hate the beach, unless it's piled up with stinking seaweed, or there's a storm going on. I love a good storm. It makes such a miserable mess."

Drizzle looked thoughtful when the Craggy Crow told her about the children helping to put up their tents. He hadn't noticed the fairies, but he'd seen how small some of the children were.

"Small humans, you say? Good! They'll be really easy to upset," Drizzle sneered. "You crows must visit the dear little kiddies. I want you to teach them a new game. It's called 'terrifying tents'!"

Back at Silvershell Bay, night had fallen. All the children were asleep in their tents, and so were *most* of the fairies. But Daisy the Dream Fairy was still wide awake, and was sitting outside with her three sleepy friends. She was pointing to the stars.

"When we're at the seaside, we Dream Fairies like to look at the stars," she explained. "Did you know, they all have two names – a fairy name and a human name?" She began to point out some of her favourites.

"I'd love to give a star a name," Sophie sighed, and gave a great big yawn.

"Me, too. But now I'm too sleepy to think of one," Freya added, rubbing her eyes drowsily.

"Sorry, Daisy," Clara said. "I'm going to have to go to bed, before I fall asleep right here on the ground!"

Soon, Daisy was the only fairy left awake outside, but she didn't mind. She was so happy star-watching on her own, when suddenly she heard a noise. It was the sound of somebody crying, and it was coming from the humans' campsite.

As Daisy flew closer, she heard more sniffles and sobs, and soon she saw why.

Several Craggy Crows were strutting around in the light of a campfire, their wings outstretched to make shadows on the sides of the tents. To the frightened children inside, the shadows looked like big, scary monsters. The mean crows were throwing in a few monster-style screeches, too.

"Hey, go away!" cried Daisy, but the crows didn't even notice her.

Angrily, she flew back to the fairy camp.

"Wake up, wake up!" she cried. "Quickly! The humans need our help, NOW!"

Chapter 4

Trouble Ahead

"Please wake up!" Daisy cried. Her three friends stirred and rubbed their eyes, still half-asleep.

"The Craggy Crows are scaring the children. We must do something!" Daisy urged, anxiously. That woke Freya, Sophie and Clara up fast. The four friends slipped on their backpacks containing their trusty spells. They rushed to the human school campsite, which was in turmoil. The Craggy Crows had gone, but many of the children were still upset and crying.

"There's a monster outside!"

"I want my mummy!"

The teachers were trying to settle everyone down, but it wasn't working.

Sophie quickly delved into her backpack to find her Birthday Fairy Magic Beauty Jewel. She held it up and whispered:

"Weave a pretty musical spell,
Make the children feel safe and well."

Soft lullaby music floated over the camp and began to calm everyone down. Meanwhile, Freya flew secretly from tent to tent wearing her Fashion Fairy Good Feeling Spell Ring. It had the power to give people happy thoughts.

Freya murmured a spell under her breath:

"Think about playing in the sun.
Dream about some seaside fun."

Daisy and Clara flew off to find Mrs Daffodil. By the time the three of them returned, the fairy magic of the jewel and the ring had worked. The campsite had grown quiet, as everybody fell back to sleep.

"Well done, everybody," Mrs Daffodil whispered. "Now we must get some rest, too. Off to sleep, little fairies!"

Daisy made a face and moaned. "But I don't think I can sleep now!"

"Us, too!" the others agreed. After all the fuss and bother at the campsite, the fairies felt wide awake. Mrs Daffodil waved her hand gently, and softly muttered a sleeping spell:

"Time to snuggle in your beds,
And rest your little fairy heads."

The four friends all began to yawn at the same time.

"Now I'm tired!" Freya said.

"Us, too," the others agreed. They returned to their cosy tent, slipped under their flower petals and quickly fell asleep. Even Daisy!

The next day, the fairies did all they could to make the children's school trip a happy one. Sophie sprinkled her Clever Weather Magic Dust over the beach, to make the sun shine. The children and teachers spilled on to the sand for a day of games and picnicking, and Daisy used her Spell Ring magic to make everything taste dreamy.

The fairies hid behind a sandcastle to watch the fun.

"Mmmm — I have never tasted such wonderful food," they heard a teacher remark. "This cake is out of this world!"

The fairies giggled. "Out of fairyland, she means!"

The rest of their time at Silvershell Bay passed smoothly, with no more visits from the Craggy Crows. But, on the way home, Mrs Daffodil gave them all a warning.

"The Craggy Crows caused a lot of upset on the trip. Thanks to Daisy, we have been able to stop it going too far, but Drizzle's potion will have gained power from all the unhappiness. Watch out, fairies, there could be trouble ahead!"

Chapter 5

A Storm Hits

Mrs Daffodil was right. Back in Stinky Swamp, Drizzle's magic potion had started to bubble as soon as the children had begun to cry in their tents. It turned from its usual green to a muddy brown colour, which showed that it was sucking up a lot of power very quickly. The witch cackled in triumph:

"Lovely, smelly, bubbly potion,
Let's put an evil spell in motion!"

By the time the Craggy Crows returned from Silvershell Bay, her cackle sounded meaner than ever.

"Your little visit to the kiddies has given me a wickedly good idea. I'm going to brew up a storm! We haven't had a good one for ages, or should I say a *bad* one?"

She took a small bottle from her pocket and began to fill it with potion. It was about half full when she screeched angrily.

"Aaaargh! My potion! It's stopped bubbling. You didn't make the humans unhappy enough!" she shrieked at the Craggy Crows. Sure enough, the smelly mixture in the cauldron had turned back to its usual dull green, and was no longer splashing. Only the liquid in Drizzle's bottle stayed brown and bubbly.

"Wait a minute...did you see any fairies at Silvershell Bay?" she demanded, crossly. The Craggy Crows cowered, too scared to reply.

"There must have been fairies! They must have cheered up the dratted children," she spat. "Well, I've got enough brown potion to make a storm over at least *one* place. I'll choose a pretty fairy spot to wreck. That'll teach those little do-gooders!"

Drizzle waited for the next cloudy evening to do her worst. Clutching her bottle, she headed to the prettiest fairy spot she knew – Moonbeam Lake. High up and hidden from view, she poured potion into the air as she hissed out a storm spell.

Gales and rainshowers...
whip up a storm!

Thunder and lightning...
do some harm!

Daisy had her three friends staying for a sleepover that evening. They were all out by the lake, practising their flying skills together, when the storm hit.

43

CRACK!

CRACK!

The wind whistled across the water.
Crack! A tree branch fell down into the
lake, narrowly missing a family of frogs.
Splash! Another fell. It scattered ducks
and ducklings.

SPLASH!

PLOP!

"Quickly! Get back to the clock tower!" Daisy shouted above the noise. The fairies battled their way through the wind to the shelter of the tower. Daisy rushed inside to get her mum, but all she found was a note on the kitchen table.

"Popped out to pick up your little sister. Back in ten minutes," she read. "It's no good! I'm going to have to sort this one out myself!"

The friends watched helplessly as the storm whipped up waves and damaged trees around the lakeside. The lake animals began to panic.

"I'm fed up with Drizzle picking on things smaller than her!" Daisy cried angrily. She opened her backpack and grabbed a big handful of her special Clever Weather Dust.

"Dream Fairy dust has the power to calm storms," she explained. "I'll need to fly up above the clouds, to sprinkle it around."

Her friends gasped as lightning flashed across the sky above them.

"It's horrible up there! Be careful!"

Daisy flew off into the pelting rain. "I will be," she called, and flew higher and higher, until her friends lost sight of her.

Chapter 6
Stop that Fairy!

Daisy flew up into the storm clouds, where an eerie mist swirled around her. She tried not to think of the lightning that might flash past her at any moment.

She muttered to herself, "Keep flying, keep flying."

Suddenly, she burst out above the clouds into the nighttime darkness above. That's when Drizzle saw her!

"A fairy!" the witch screamed. "Quick! Chase her!"

The Craggy Crows flew towards the little fairy, followed by Drizzle, urging them on.

"Stop that fairy now! She's out to ruin my storm!"

Daisy felt scared, but she also felt angry at the thought of all her animal friends having their homes wrecked by the wind and rain.

She shouted defiantly back at Drizzle, "You can try all you like, but you can't catch a Dream Fairy!"

It was true. Dream Fairies are fantastic fliers, and although the Craggy Crows were fast, they were nowhere near as skilful in the air as Daisy. She zigzagged, swooped and looped-the-loop in front of them, gradually tiring them out. All the while, she let Clever Weather Dust slip through her fingers, to drift down on to the clouds below.

Drizzle was soon huffing and puffing, tired by the chase, but she kept shouting at her gang of crows.

"What are you – courageous crows or cowardly creeps? Don't let a fairy get the better of you!"

The crows made one last big effort and almost caught up with Daisy. She could hear their wings beating close behind her. She swerved downwards, but saw a couple of birds flying below her. The only way to escape was to go up!

"Here goes!" she cried, and zoomed upwards like a miniature space rocket, higher than any bird could follow.

Up and up she sped, until the calls of the crows and the screeches of the witch grew faint below her. At last, she slowed down, safe from her enemies.

"Phew! Time to go home now," she thought. "But how?" It was very dark and very quiet. The stars looked different up high, and Daisy didn't recognise them. Which way was home?

Daisy looked around and sighed. "Oh dear. I'm lost."

She reached into her backpack and clutched her Magic Beauty Jewel. Holding it up in the darkness, she chanted a Dream Fairy spell:

"Shine on me a silver star's light,
To brighten up the darkest night."

A trail of starlight streamed from the jewel, but although it was beautiful, it was not bright enough to show poor Daisy the way home.

Chapter 7

To the Rescue

Back at Moonbeam Lake, Daisy's friends were getting worried.

At first, they'd cheered when they saw her Clever Weather Dust do its work. As soon as she had sprinkled it over the stormclouds, they had melted away. The storm stopped as quickly as it had started, and the three fairies sped busily around the lake, helping to tidy up.

Sophie had the special Birthday Fairy skill of being able to speak to animals.

She explained to all the lake creatures what had happened. They all thought Daisy was very brave and stayed out, ready to thank her when she returned. But they waited and waited, and there was no sign of her.

"What could have happened to her?" Freya cried.

Clara frowned. "I don't know, but we can't wait for Daisy's mum to get back. We need to go up ourselves and look for Daisy, now!"

Sophie shook her head. "But we're not Dream Fairies. The three of us can't fly that well at nighttime."

"I know," muttered Clara. "But we must think of a way." She was a Clever Fairy, so she was great at making plans.

"I've got it!" she cried. "We can't fly up on our own, but I know four little bats who could help!"

Freya clapped her hands. "Itsy, Bitsy, Batso and Bottletop! Of course! Daisy's pets are fantastic night fliers."

"Exactly," Clara grinned.

Sophie zipped off into the clock tower and soon returned with Daisy's four furry bat friends. She explained to them exactly what had happened, and they squeaked excitedly.

Sophie translated their animal language for her friends. "They're saying 'Hop aboard'. They'll take us higher and faster than we could ever hope to fly all by ourselves."

The three fairies climbed on to Itsy, Bitsy and Bottletop. Batso flew ahead, looking out for any trouble. It grew darker and colder as they rose up into the night sky. Thankfully, there was no sign of Drizzle or her crows. They'd gone home to Stinky Swamp, exhausted. But there was no sign of Daisy either.

The little bats squeaked to each other.

"They're saying they're sure Daisy is somewhere nearby," Sophie explained to the others. "But she's gone very high and she's probably lost. Hang on tightly. We're going up!"

The fairies and bats sped upwards into the darkness. Suddenly Clara cried out.

"Over there! There's something shining and it's not a star – it's moving. Daisy! Daisy! Is that you?"

As Daisy shone her beam of starlight around, she heard Clara's voice.

"Over here!" she called. Then the rescue party appeared at her side.

"Am I glad to see you!" Daisy cried.

"Are you okay?" Clara asked.

"Just a bit tired and cold, and more than ready to go home," Daisy smiled, climbing on to Batso and giving him a big hug.

Chapter 8
Clara's Clever Plan

The bats flew the fairies safely back down to Moonbeam Lake. Daisy's mum was back by now, and she was horrified to hear what chaos Drizzle had caused while she was away. She gave Daisy a big cuddle for being so brave, and she made everyone a cup of hot chocolate to warm them all up, after their chilly night flight.

It took a while for the four friends to get to sleep in the clock tower that night.

All the little creatures who lived around the lake came to thank Daisy for managing to stop the storm. Frogs, ducks, birds, wild bats and all kinds of tiny insects turned up at the door. It was quite a noisy evening!

The next morning, the fairies could see there was still a lot of clearing up to do around the lake.

Daisy frowned angrily. "It makes me so mad! I'd like to teach Drizzle a lesson!"

They hurried off to school and told Mrs Daffodil what had happened. She took the whole class to Moonbeam Lake to help clear up.

After they'd finished, the fairies sat down by the lake for a well-earned rest. Daisy's friends noticed that she was smiling to herself.

"Come on, spill the beans!" Freya laughed. "We can tell you've thought of something good!"

Daisy nodded. "Well, first we need to check with Mrs Daffodil, and ask for her help…but I think I've come up with a way to give Drizzle a taste of her own medicine, and it'll be fun!"

Freya grinned. "Brilliant! Where do we start?"

"The Craggy Crows gave me the idea," Daisy explained. "Remember when they scared the children with their shadows? The light of the campfire made the shadows look really big and scary. So, I was wondering what kind of shadow might scare Drizzle…"

"Something that's bigger than her?" Sophie guessed.

"Something with more powerful magic than her?" Clara suggested.

"Something even meaner than her?" Freya added.

"Exactly!" Daisy grinned. "How about making some bigger, cleverer, meaner witches, out to steal her potion?"

"Fantastic!"

The class gathered in a huddle, and Daisy whispered her plan. When they told Mrs Daffodil, she laughed and agreed to help.

"Tell your parents what we're going to do," she told the class. "And tomorrow, bring in all the spare cardboard you can find. We're going to need it to create our surprise!"

Chapter 9
All About Witches

The next morning, school began with a fascinating lesson from Mrs Daffodil, all about Drizzle's witch enemies.

"Drizzle isn't the only witch in the world," she explained. "There are quite a few others. But luckily for us, witches hate each other even more than they hate fairies! They live as far away from each other as they can, and if they ever meet up, they fight and try to steal each other's potions."

Freya pulled a face. "What a horrid, grumpy bunch."

Mrs Daffodil nodded. "Yes, they're all as bad-tempered as Drizzle, but some of them are bigger and more powerful than her. She'd be scared of them if they turned up. Have a look at the pictures in my witch books."

The fairies gathered round to look at Mrs Daffodil's books – *The Spotter's Guide to Witches* and *The Atlas of Horrible Hags*.

Freya pointed to a picture. "This one's called Gertie Grot. It says that her dad was a giant, so she's as tall as a tree. And her hobby is fighting!"

"There's one on this page called Wartie," added Sophie. "Apparently, she's known for having spiky hair and big ears and she's a black belt at karate!"

Clara joined in. "And how about Aggie Screech? It says here that she holds the record for being the most bad-tempered witch in the world, and for having the biggest hat."

Mrs Daffodil smiled. "These three sound perfect. Shall we begin?"

The fairies started drawing, cutting up card and sticking bits and pieces together. Every now and then, they would look back at the pictures in the books. By the end of the day they had made three large cardboard witch shapes that looked just like the awful outlines of Gertie Grot, Wartie and Aggie Screech.

Now all the fairies had to do was wait patiently for nighttime. They needed darkness for their trick to work.

"We've had a lot of nighttime adventures in the last few days. Everyone is going to be late to bed again," Daisy pointed out. "But if this trick works, Drizzle won't be around to bother us for ages. We'll be able to take it easy for a while!"

"Now, is everyone ready?" asked Mrs Daffodil, when it was dark outside. The fairies noticed that she had something unusual in her hand. It looked a little bit like a tiny silver trumpet.

"It's a witchaphone," she explained, but she just smiled mysteriously when the fairies asked her what it did.

"You'll see!"

Suddenly, there was a noise outside the classroom window. It was the soft beating of wings.

"The bats are here!" Daisy declared. Itsy, Bitsy, Batso and Bottletop were outside, with quite a few friends. Lots

of the wild bats that lived around Moonbeam Lake had come, too, along with some of the nighttime moths.

Mrs Daffodil organised everyone into three teams, one in charge of each cardboard witch shape.

"Everybody into position," she ordered.
"One, two, three…lift!"

Between them, the bats, moths and
fairies lifted the models up into the air.
The school doors were flung open wide,
and they all flew off into the night.

Chapter 10

Drizzle Gets a Visit

All was quiet in the streets below. The humans had gone to bed, which was lucky, because if they'd looked up they'd have been surprised to see three weird witch shapes in the sky!

The fairies and their friends headed for the edge of Stinky Swamp. Each team worked together to make their model swoop up and down, just like a real witch flying around looking for trouble.

Clara's team were carrying Gertie Grot,

and Sophie's team were working Wartie. Freya's team made Aggie Screech dive and then zoom upwards again.

"Go, Aggie!' she whispered excitedly.

Daisy and Mrs Daffodil hid themselves out of sight in the branches of a tree. Daisy took out her Magic Beauty Jewel and quietly began to chant a Dream Fairy spell:

"Shine some silvery, twinkly starlight,
To help make shadows in the night."

A ray of starlight streamed from the jewel and helped the cardboard witches to make big scary shadows that flitted across the trees and bushes around the edge of the swamp. There was no mistaking who they were supposed to be!

Mrs Daffodil held her witchaphone to her lips. Daisy noticed that it had two buttons on it, marked 'mean voice' and 'scary cackle'. Mrs Daffodil pressed the cackle button and laughed softly into the witchaphone. A cackle came out that was so loud, it echoed all around Stinky Swamp!

It worked beautifully. Drizzle quickly appeared. As soon as she saw the witch shadows flitting around in the darkness, she screamed and began to panic.

"Gertie Grot! Wartie! Aggie Screech! Get away from my swamp, you horrible hags! You'll never get your warty hands on my potion!"

Mrs Daffodil pressed the mean voice button on her witchaphone and began to whisper into it. A voice came out that sounded like an old witch, shouting.

"We're coming to get you, Drizzle. We want your potion!"

"Never!" Drizzle squealed. "Nobody's getting their hands on MY potion!" She fled back to her cauldron, took hold of one edge, and heaved it over. With a gloopy, slurping sound, the potion poured out on to the ground and seeped away into the swamp.

The fairies' parents were waiting for them when they got back to school. Everyone clapped and cheered when they heard about Drizzle being tricked into pouring away her chaos potion.

"It'll take her weeks to cook up a new one from scratch," Clara grinned.

Freya gave Daisy a big hug. "It was fun staying up tonight," she said.

Sophie agreed. "I'm getting quite used to all this flying in the dark."

"Good," said Daisy. "Because we Dream Fairies have got one more surprise planned for tonight, and we want everyone to come!"

All the Utterly Flutterly Fairies flew to Moonbeam Lake. They found it bathed in a magical Dream Fairy starlight.

There was dreamy-tasting picnic food for everybody, and a roaring campfire to sit by.

"There are loads of reasons why I like nighttime," Daisy explained, between mouthfuls of toasted marshmallows and hot chocolate. "There's the stars, the moonbeams, and there's nighttime flying with my bat friends. What do you think?" she asked her friends.

Freya, Sophie and Clara didn't reply. All three were huddled snugly by the fire, fast asleep!

Utterly Flutterly Quiz

Each Utterly Flutterly Fairy lives in a very special house. What would yours be like?

1. Which of these would you like your house to be?

A. Somewhere up high with amazing views
B. Snug, secret and cosy (and a little bit magical, too!)
C. Tucked away near the ground, with lots of flowers
D. Beautiful, old and with a pretty pond in your back garden

2. Which of the following appeals to you most?

A. A leaf
B. A wish
C. A flower
D. A lake

3. What would your fairy house be made from?

A. *Wood and leaves*
B. *Brick, with a thatched roof*
C. *Rocks and plants*
D. *Stone and marble*

4. Which of these would your house be near?

A. *A leafy park*
B. *Sophie's house*
C. *The human school*
D. *Daisy's house*

5. Which pet would you choose?

A. *A squirrel*
B. *A bird*
C. *A frog*
D. *A fish*

Utterly Flutterly Quiz Answers

Now check your answers to find out what your fairy house would be:

Mostly As: Up high in the branches of a magnificent oak tree, in the most beautiful park in the human town.

Mostly Bs: Inside an empty bird's nest, beneath the canopy of a wishing well, in the same garden as Sophie's house.

Mostly Cs: Tucked between the stones of the human school's garden rockery, surrounded by pretty flowers.

Mostly Ds: Tucked beneath the ledge of a beautiful old fountain, in the middle of a pond near Daisy's house on Moonbeam Lake.

Utterly Flutterly Anagrams

Drizzle the Wicked Witch has been causing mischief by muddling up these words so that no one can read them. Can you sort them out and work out what they should say? Turn the page upside down to see if you're right.

plottobet

mared

hingmidt

pigmnac ript

asyid

stoab

oboneamm kale

vilhersells aby

yitsb

ratss

Answers:

plottobet: bottletop, *mared:* dream, *hingmidt:* midnight, *pigmnac ript:* camping trip, *asyid:* daisy, *stoab:* batso, *oboneamm kale:* moonbeam lake, *vilhersells aby:* silvershell bay, *yitsb:* bitsy, *ratss:* stars

85

Daisy's dreamy hot chocolate

Utterly Flutterly Fairies love to drink dreamy hot chocolate. Here's how you can make your very own delicious drink.

Ingredients

1 litre/1¾ pints of milk
150g/5½oz plain chocolate
Sugar, to taste
Whipped cream (optional)
Cocoa powder (optional)
Marshmallows (optional)

Kit

Saucepan, whisk, wooden spoon, mugs

1. Break the chocolate into small pieces and put to one side.

2. Pour the milk into a saucepan and ask an adult to help you carefully bring it to the boil.

REMEMBER! ALWAYS ASK AN ADULT TO HELP YOU WHEN USING THE COOKER!

3. Carefully add the chocolate to the milk and stir constantly until all the chocolate has melted.

4. Whisk the chocolatey mixture until it has a good froth on top.

5. Add sugar until the mixture tastes sweet enough, and serve in mugs. Add whipped cream to the top and dust with cocoa powder.

Fairy Tip: Add marshmallows to make your drink even dreamier.

spooky sleepover z z N z

Here's how to throw a great spooky sleepover for your friends!

Invite your friends over to stay and ask them to bring sleeping bags, pillows, pyjamas and any spooky stories they have.

Before your friends arrive, decorate the room you're going to sleep in with spooky decorations. Try cutting out bats from a piece of black paper and putting them up on the walls. (Remember to ask an adult first and be careful when using scissors.)

Once everyone has arrived, arrange your sleeping bags and pillows so that you each have a comfy make-shift bed.

Make some delicious hot chocolate using the recipe on pages 86–87 and prepare some tasty snacks for a midnight feast.

Get into your sleeping bags, sit in a circle and tell each other spooky stories, or turn to page 92 to learn how to write your own...

Fairy code words!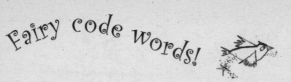

You can make up fairy code words by taking each letter from a word and using it to start another word like this:

Dreamy   **D**ream   **M**ysterious

Awesome   **R**emarkable   **I**ntriguing

Imaginative   **E**nchanting   **D**ark

Splendid   **A**mazing   **N**octurnal

Yawn free   **M**agical   **I**ncredible

                                       Ghostly

                                       Haunting

                                       Twilight

More word ideas!

Why don't you try making up a fairy code word using your own name? Here are some words to get you started:

Nice

Friendly

Lucky

Happy

Smiley

Jolly

Chirpy

Optimistic

Polite

Brave

How to write spooky sleepover stories

This game is great for sleepovers and can be played by two or more people.

You will need:

 Paper

 Pens

A good imagination

1. Sit in a circle with your friends and choose someone to write down the first line of a spooky story.

2. The person must then fold over the page so that no-one can read it, and pass it to the person sitting to their right.

3. This person must write another line for the story, fold over the page and pass it on to the person sitting to *their* right.

4. Carry on until everyone has had a go. (If your circle is small, go round two or three times.)

5. The last person to go must write an ending line for the story.

6. Unfold the paper and ask the person who wrote the first line to read the story out loud.

Fairy Tip: Choose a different theme each time — how about fairytales, adventure or mystery? Or why not try basing your story on the Utterly Flutterly Fairies?

Look out for these
Utterly Flutterly titles!

Utterly Flutterly Fairies

Sophie
the
Birthday Fairy

Moira Butterfield

Utterly Flutterly Fairies

Clara
the
Clever Fairy

Moira Butterfield

Utterly Flutterly Fairies

Freya
the
Fashion Fairy

Moira Butterfield